Kerstin Hau lives in Darmstadt, Germany, where she was born. She has worked in many different fields, including physiotherapy, fitness training, and specialist journalism. She graduated from the Academy for Children's Media and had a son of her own. She has learned that in life everything new emerges from darkness and true love never dies. This is the material from which she weaves her stories. Since 2015 she has been freelance writing for children and grown-ups.

Julie Völk was born in Vienna, Austria. She later moved to Hamburg, North Germany, where she studied illustration at the University of Applied Sciences. Her pictures tell stories about growing up, strange meetings, and unusual aspects of life; and her clear, delicate style combines realism with fantasy, which gives her illustrations a highly original atmosphere. She now lives and works just outside Vienna.

First published in the United States, Great Britain, Canada, Australia, and New Zealand in 2019 by NorthSouth Books, Inc., an imprint of NordSüd Verlag AG, CH-8050 Zürich, Switzerland.

Distributed in the United States by NorthSouth Books, Inc., New York 10016.
Library of Congress Cataloging-in-Publication Data is available.
ISBN: 978-0-7358-4385-1 (trade edition)

1 3 5 7 9 · 10 8 6 4 2
Printed in Livonia Print, Riga, Latvia, March 2019
www.northsouth.com

by Kerstin Hau   illustrated by Julie Völk

THE DARK
AND THE LIGHT

Translated by David Henry Wilson

North
South

Shaggy crouched in the darkness,
looking across at the place of shining colors.

"Oh, if only I could go there! If only I knew
how! But I can't do it on my own."

He sighed, and his heart felt heavy.

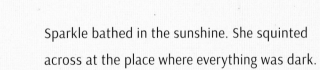

Sparkle bathed in the sunshine. She squinted
across at the place where everything was dark.

"Ugh, how dark and gloomy it is!
I wouldn't want to go there.
But I'm curious all the same."

Shaggy was brave.
He put on his rubber boots
and plodded toward the sunshine.

"I'll just go to the edge
of the darkness,
have a quick look,
and then come back."

Sparkle was brave.
She picked up a flashlight
and walked toward the darkness.

"I'll just go to the edge
of the light,
have a quick look,
and then come back."

Shaggy stood at the edge of the darkness and saw silhouettes in the bright light.
Sparkle stood at the edge of the light and saw two eyes in the darkness.

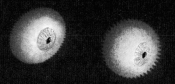

They both stood there for a long
time looking at each other.
Then Shaggy disappeared into the night,
where there was not a glimmer to be seen,
and Sparkle returned to the colors.

The next day they met again. And they
met again the day after that.

"Hello, you there in the light.
Who are you?"
asked Shaggy.

Sparkle was startled. WHOOSH! Away she ran.
Many of us are afraid of the dark.

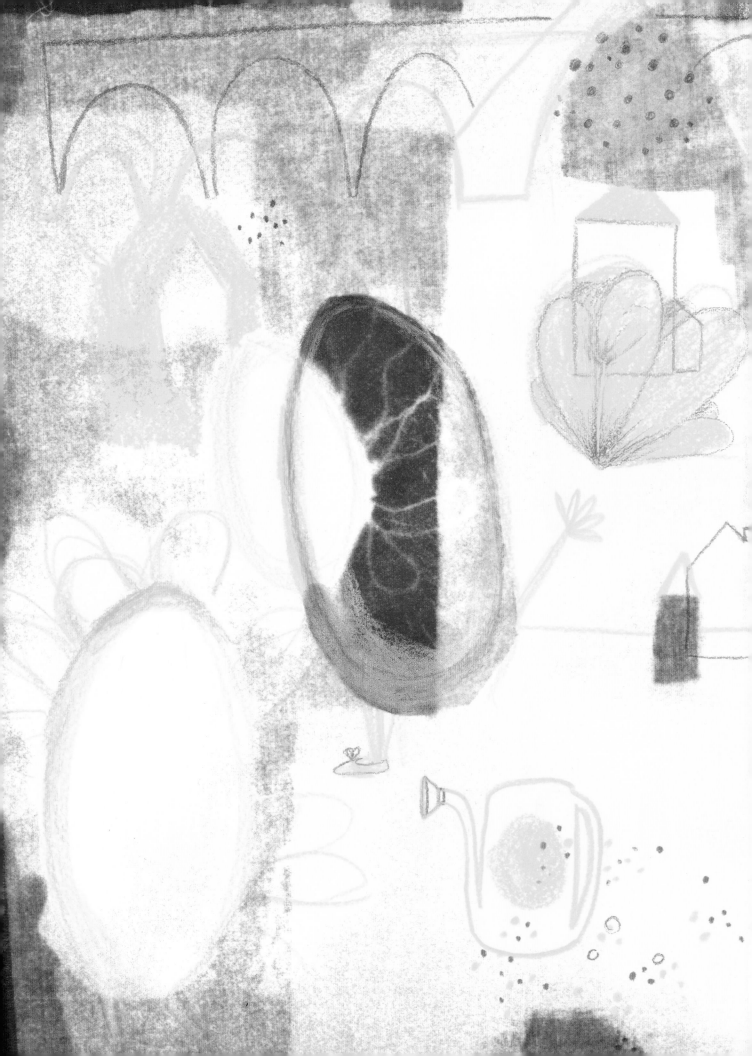

The next day Shaggy waited for Sparkle.

She didn't come.

Shaggy's head dropped.

"I'll come here again tomorrow,
but it will be the last time."

When Shaggy came to the border for the
last time, Sparkle was already waiting there.

"Hello, you there in the dark.
Who are you?"
she asked in a trembling voice. Her little heart
was so nervous that it fluttered like a butterfly.

"Me? I'm Shaggy. And you?"
"I'm Sparkle. Will you be my friend?"
she asked as her knees shook.
"Me? Your friend? Yes, I'd love that!"
said Shaggy with a smile,
and his joyful heart leaped like a frog.
He had been wishing and wishing
he could have a friend.

At the border it was neither dark nor light. There
was a band of gray-blue—half light and half dark.

Sparkle entered the band for the first time.
Shaggy entered the band for the first time.
In the excitement, the hairs on their necks stood on
end. They tickled like the tiny legs of a hundred insects.

"It's nice to have
a friend like you,"
said Shaggy,
who was now closer to the colors
than he had ever been before.

"It's nice to have
a friend like you,"
said Sparkle, who was
now closer to the darkness
than she had ever been before.

From now on the two of them
met every day.

One day, and only for a moment, Shaggy dared to go with Sparkle
into the light. Of course he took a parasol with him.
Sparkle held Shaggy's hand and said, "Don't be afraid. I'm here with you."

Shaggy was not at all afraid,
because he had a friend beside him.
All the same he was excited and wagged his little tail.

"Every day now we'll go a little farther into the shining colors,"
said Sparkle.

"Oh yes!"

said Shaggy happily. From that moment on,
bright spots began to appear on his dark coat.

"Do you think your coat will grow completely light?"

"No, the darkness can never leave the coat completely.

But a spotted coat is very beautiful," said Shaggy.

"That's true," said Sparkle.

One day Shaggy waited and waited for Sparkle.
"Where can she be?" he wondered,
and scratched his head.
After a while he said:
"I must go and find her. All on my own."
With determined steps, he walked
through the gray-blue band.

jumped across

he

Then

the edge of

the light

and stood before the laughing sun.
Shaggy was very proud of himself as he hurried
toward his friend's house.

"Sparkle! I'm here!
I made it!"

"OH!"

Shaggy stood
as if rooted to the spot,
his eyes wide
with shock.

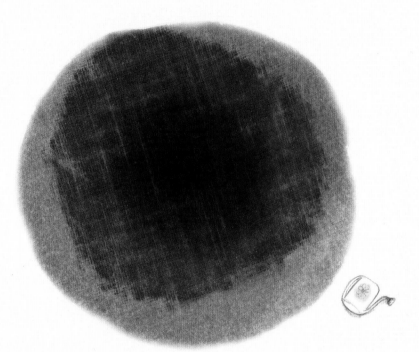

His friend's house had disappeared! Nothing was left.
All that remained to show that something had once been there
was a large, deep hole that split the ground like an open wound.

Shaggy raced home
as fast as he could, back into
the heart of the darkness.

"Oh dear! Oh dear!"
he moaned.

But when Shaggy reached his
house, his mouth fell wide
open in sheer amazement.

"It's you!" he cried. "You're here!"
To his great joy, he found Sparkle
standing outside his front door.
But then he saw that his
friend was crying.

"What happened?"

"Something swallowed up my house!
Suddenly everything went dark,"
sobbed Sparkle, and her bright coat
grew darker with every tear.

Shaggy held his
friend very tightly.
"That was how I felt too."

"I'm frightened.
It's all so strange!" wept Sparkle.

"I know," said Shaggy. "There are
lots of eyes to look at you, and
claws to clutch at you, and toads to
croak at you; but you'll get used to
them. And they won't hurt you.

"We're friends, and we'll get through this together."

"Yes," sniffled Sparkle.
She couldn't say any more.

Gradually she got used to the gloomy darkness, and soon she didn't even
need her flashlight. The friends played hide-and-seek or tag with the
croaking toads and the owners of the eyes and claws. The toads
and clawed creatures really were quite harmless.

One day Shaggy said to Sparkle,
"Today we'll go back to the gray-blue band."
"Really?" said Sparkle hesitantly.
"Really," said Shaggy with a smile.

Hand in hand they set off.
For a long time they stood looking across at the colors.
Then they went back into the darkness.

One day, and only for a moment,
Sparkle dared to go back into the light again
with Shaggy. They took a parasol, of course.

Shaggy held Sparkle's hand and said,
"Don't be afraid. I'm here with you."

Sparkle was not at all afraid
because she had a friend beside her.
All the same she was excited
and wagged her little tail.

"Let's do this every day now,"
said Shaggy.

"Oh yes,"
said Sparkle happily, and from that moment on,
bright spots began to appear on her darkened coat.

After a few visits the two friends built a new house in the place of shining colors.

But they also kept their other house back in the darkness.

They were not at all afraid of the dark.

They both agreed that there was nothing better
in the whole world than to have a friend who
understood the need for a parasol and a flashlight.

CYANOTYPE

The pictures in this book were made with
a special technique called cyanotype.
Cyanotype is one of the very first processes
used in photography. It was invented in
1842 by the English scientist and astronomer
Sir John Herschel. A typical feature of this
technique is the different, intense shades
of blue.

If you would like to try using the technique for yourself, you need specially prepared paper known as solar or sun print paper. You can get this in any shop that sells artists' materials or in some DIY shops.

You will need to work in a darkened room. You can put all kinds of objects on the paper, for example, flowers and leaves, buttons, or different papers and materials. Or you can draw something with a black edding pen on transparent foil.

When you have everything ready on the solar paper, take it outside and lay it in the sunshine.

In good weather, the process will need between three and six minutes, but if the weather is cloudy you should leave it for a bit longer.

In order to stop the objects from sliding off or being blown away, you can use a picture frame with the glass covering the objects.

When the paper has absorbed the light, take it back into the darkened room and rinse it thoroughly with clean water. The best way is to put it under the shower.

After that, all you have to do is leave it to dry. During the next few hours the blue tone will intensify. When the paper is dry, the picture will be imprinted on it.